Monster and the Magic Umbrella

Monster and the Magic Umbrella

Ellen Blance and
Ann Cook
wrote this story.

Quentin Blake drew the pictures.

SCHOLASTIC BOOK SERVICES
NEW YORK · TORONTO · LONDON · AUCKLAND · SYDNEY · TOKYO

Text copyright © 1973 by Ann Cook and Ellen Blance. Illustrations copyright © 1973 by Longman Group Limited, London. This edition is published by Scholastic Book Services, a division of Scholastic Magazines, Inc., by arrangement with Bowmar Publishing Corporation, Glendale, California.

12 11 10 9 8 7 6 5 4   7 8 9/7 0 1/8

Printed in the U.S.A.

This book belongs to

_____

One day Monster
and the little boy
got out of bed.
The day was so hot.
The sun was shining.
So Monster said,
"Come on, let's wash up
and get dressed
so we can go outside
and play."

So that's what they did.
It was such a hot day.
So Monster got his best hat
and his umbrella
to keep the sun off
his face.

P. 6

Then everyone played ball.
The sun was shining
on them.
They smelled sweaty.

Then all the boys
and all the girls went off.
Their mothers called them
for dinner.
Monster and the little boy
felt so hot.
The little boy said,
"Oh, Monster,
I feel so hot."

So Monster opened
the umbrella
to keep the sun off
their faces.
"Now it'll be much cooler,"
Monster said.
So that's what Monster did.

He just opened his umbrella.
Then the umbrella grew
bigger . . .

. . . and bigger.

Then Monster turned it
around.
Boy, wasn't it giant-sized!
Super big!
So the little boy
and Monster just looked.
Then the little boy said,
"Oh, Monster,
I wish we had
a swimming pool
to swim in.
I'm so hot."

Suddenly
big drops of water
fell in the umbrella.
Then the little boy said,
"Oh boy!
Doesn't that look
like a swimming pool!
Let's take off our socks
and shoes and jump in
and take a swim."
Monster said,
"Yeah, why not."

The water was all cool.
It felt so good.

The boys and girls
came back out.
All the boys
and all the girls
took their shoes off.
They jumped in
and just splashed the water
up and down.
Up and down.

Then, "Home for bed,
home for bed,"
everybody said.
Everybody said,
"Let's do that tomorrow.
That's really fun."

So the umbrella
got smaller and smaller
and tinier and tinier.

Then the umbrella wasn't
a magic umbrella anymore.
Then Monster
and the little boy
went to their house
to go to bed.
The little boy said,
"Maybe we can do that
tomorrow, Monster."
So Monster said,
"Yeah, maybe we can."